Beyond the Pale

BRÝN GROVER

Beyond the Pale

Printed edition ISBN: 979-8-9908001-2-0

Published by Brýn's Quill

DEDICATION

For this collection of short stories, I want to dedicate each of them individually.

Audrey's Leg is dedicated to Dan

Rejection Proof is dedicated to Angel H-G

Flower Ceremony is dedicated to Tharzill

New Glasses is dedicated to Charles W

Cabin Getaway is dedicated to Tory

The Fisherman is dedicated to Tiffini because if anything ever happens, I'll be employing his services

Saying Goodbye is dedicated to Mike D

The Wasting is dedicated to Bryan N

Starting Over is dedicated to the memory of Dean

The Penny Farthing is dedicated to Paul S

FOREWORD

We've always known monsters lurk in the shadows. Terror waits in abandoned houses and misty graveyards. But horror also loves flowers at funerals, wears scrubs in hospital corridors, and rides a bike.

Welcome to Beyond the Pale, where U.S. Army veteran Brýn Grover invites you to discover the darkness that lives side-by-side with the familiar. This collection of ten tales refuses to separate fear into neat categories.

Some stories delve into the macabre or paranormal, while others meld science fiction with nightmares. Whether following characters through routine experiences or watching them confront impossible circumstances, each story reveals how thin the membrane is between tranquility and terror.

The phrase "beyond the pale" refers to something outside the bounds of morality. Prepare yourself to cross those boundaries. In these tales, even time can become the enemy.

— Charles Wood

Author of *The Girl Who Sleeps in the Room Next to Me*

CONTENTS

ACKNOWLEDGMENTS

Of course, anything that ever gets done in my writing always has one inexorable force behind it, the support and primary cheerleader that is my wyfe (not a typo or spell check issue but a purposeful spelling I use). So, I must give her the credit she is due. Thank you Tiffini!

I'd also like to acknowledge Charles Wood and Bryan Nowak for their continued support and encouragement.

1 AUDREY'S LEG

Pain and a sense of intense loss overcame Audrey as she awakened to see her left foot cut off above the ankle. The pain throbbed even though she was on medication. With each beat of her heart, the pain spiked. It became so unbearable she succumbed to unconsciousness.

Audrey wasn't out of anesthesia yet. Unready for a recovery room, she remained where she was. Marvin looked on from a corner of the operating room. The procedures were necessary even if unpleasant.

Sometimes amputations were imperative to save a life. Audrey was in that situation. Without controlling things, her life would be forfeit. Through no desire of his own, he became the go-to person for these sessions. His bedside manner made things smoother in the long run. His experiences as a combat medic prepared him. He witnessed amputations. He comforted wounded soldiers going through this very procedure. It wasn't the job he preferred to have in the hospital, but the position did not require a lot of work. The primary duties included watching, comforting, monitoring vitals and medicines, answering questions, and escalating anything outside his realm of responsibility. The majority of it was usually watching and waiting. With patients sleeping most of the time, there wasn't much to do.

Audrey had lost her foot but she should live. Marvin watched her sleeping fitfully. She appeared to be having nightmares. He wanted to give her an additional shot of morphine. However, she had reached her maximum dosage amount already. She could not have any more for another two hours. She would have to ride it out. Marvin hoped she would remain unconscious. He hated it when the patients were screaming and he couldn't help.

He was glad he was not involved in the operating room during the procedure. He didn't mind incisions through the skin or muscle. It was the cutting of the bone that bothered him to think about. He had seen videos during training. The sounds seemed amplified. The visual was horrifying.

Knowing that a single amputation sometimes wasn't enough didn't make it better. There were rare circumstances where an additional part of a leg or arm would also get cut off.

He thought back to his friend Ned. In high school he'd been in a motorcycle accident. He lost his foot. But he didn't care for the wound afterwards. He skipped post op appointments and wallowed in his misery drinking and lamenting the loss. Infection spread. His leg got cut at mid shin. He drank more and skipped more appointments. He refused to take his antibiotics. His leg got cut again, this time at the knee. This went on until his entire leg was gone almost all the way to the hip. By the time he took things seriously, he was wheelchair bound living on disability and drinking himself into oblivion.

Unlike Ned, most patients were more likely to take proper care of themselves. Changing bandages and keeping appointments was the norm. Counselors also followed up on a regular basis to help amputees deal with the emotional effects of losing a limb. Marvin suspected Audrey would follow suit even though he didn't know her. He had a gut feeling she would struggle but nevertheless cope.

In the operating room, the monitors fed information to the nurses' station. Even so, Marvin watched them to ensure vitals remained within parameters. He was also responsible for watching the drainage and emptying the bag should it fill with fluids. Most of the time it didn't. Staples usually sealed the wound well. Even though the subfascial drain remained in place, it was rarely needed.

In essence, his primary responsibility was watching. Sit and watch. Help and comfort as needed. While he didn't want this task, it wasn't physically demanding. It could, however, take an emotional toll. It depended on the patient. Their attitude, pain level, and seriousness of the situation made all the difference. Some were easy. Others were difficult. Not knowing what you might face any given day also made it challenging.

As he sat and watched Audrey and her vitals, he found himself whistling the tune to Monty Python's song "Always Look on the Bright Side of Life." When he caught himself doing it, he smiled and chuckled. He hoped that Audrey would be able to look on the bright side of life when she regained full consciousness. No one wanted to lose a limb. She didn't even know her situation at this point. Having been in an accident and hauled into surgery unconscious, she had no inkling of what was happening.

As Audrey began to stir, the surgeon, Dr. Silverlock, came in to the operating room to check on his patient. Behind him a posse of residents with tablets were taking notes. Without saying a word, the doctor checked the chart and notated the time of his visit. He motioned for one of his residents to lift Audrey's left leg up a little higher than its current elevated point.

He inspected the bandaging and swelling in the lower extremity. Pleased with his work, he motioned for his staff to lower the leg even as Audrey tried to sit up from her prone position. Taking a step closer to her torso, he pressed a hand into her shoulder to gently force her to lay back down.

He admonished her not to make any sudden movements that could make things worse. She whimpered in pain and asked what was happening. She remembered seeing her foot gone but wasn't sure if it was a nightmare or real. But the pain was real.

Dr. Silverlock nodded to one of his residents to take the stage. He explained to Audrey that she had been in an accident and they amputated her foot to save her life and the rest of her leg. As she began to shake, Marvin was standing on the other side of the hospital bed. Taking her hand, he rubbed her forearm and tried to comfort her. He wasn't fond of this part of the job. But at least she wasn't being violent like some others had been in the past.

As the doctor and his staff left the operating room, Marvin pulled up a chair to sit next to the bed. She remained still. Crying. He sat beside her while continuing to emphasize that it would be alright. She asked for more pain medications. Marvin gave her the bad news and the schedule. She still had to wait a little bit. Dosages of narcotics were too regulated. He could not give her anything before the scheduled time. She nodded in acknowledgement. He promised to administer them when she was eligible.

Between the anesthesia from surgery and the pain, it wasn't long before Audrey fell back asleep. Marvin got up, moved his chair, and sat on the other side of the bed in view of the monitors. He waited in the quiet time wondering how she would fare. He knew it was usually a traumatic experience for the patient. Most needed only one cut. Patients requiring a second or third amputation surgery were rarer. And scarier. Despite what happened to his cousin Ned, hospital environments were different. These cases were not tied to lack of care or poor wound management like Ned's. These were other rare circumstances. He hoped this didn't apply to Audrey. Those situations were not just tough on the patient. They were hard for him and haunted him in nightmares. He hated seeing it.

As the clock hit the top of the second hour, Marvin administered more pain killers. While Audrey had not awakened, he had promised her this much. He enjoyed the peace and quiet and hoped the new dose would ease her pain and help her sleep a little longer. He knew from experience it wouldn't be too long. Once the pain subsided, the patients tended to awaken. The anesthesia would wear off. Grogginess would ensue. Once alert, the move to a recovery room would follow.

Before she awakened, Dr. Silverlock returned. Alone. Marvin's eyebrows raised in question. But he knew why. There would be another cut. The residents in this program were not brought in for the actual surgery. He watched with sadness as the doctor washed and scrubbed in for surgery. An operating room nurse and orderly followed suit.

"Unfortunately, that wasn't enough." Dr. Silverlock responded to Marvin's gaze. "We need more to save a life."

Marvin knew what this meant. That didn't make it any easier. He stepped back into a corner of the room and the procedure began. He would never get used to watching this process.

When the side door opened and it came into the room, he gasped. He'd seen it before. About the size of a black bear, it entered walking on hind legs. It had no hands or paws. It just had arms or legs that ended in pads something like an elephant's. It couldn't grip like a primate or claw like another apex predator. But it's jaws had three rows of incisors meant for ripping meat and rending prey.

Seeing it saunter in with determination made it seem even more bizarre and portentous. He thought he'd prefer an animalistic attack like a lion jumping on a wildebeest. It would be easier to take it as a part of nature. This beast was anything but natural.

Slobbering and foaming at the mouth as if afflicted with rabies, it approached the bedside. Dr. Silverlock lifted the leg. The nurse and orderly stood by prepared for surgery. The keeper of the beast stood by watching.

Without a growl, the beast bent over Audrey and opened its massive jaws. In one violent bite, her left leg was gone from mid-thigh down. As the beast stood upright and chomped its jaws around this meal, the keeper led it back into the room from which it had come.

The doctor worked at fever pitch. The nurse already had a tourniquet in place near the top of Audrey's leg close to the hip. The bone saw cut through her leg a couple inches above the ragged edges of the torn and mutilated appendage left behind by the monster. As he finished sawing, the orderly removed the damaged tissue while the doctor cauterized and stapled the wound. The nurse sanitized the leg, applied the dressing, and gathered the surgical tools to remove them.

"Is it enough? Is it satisfied?"

"Maybe. I hope so." The doctor replied to Marvin with pessimism.

"I hate this."

"We all do. But if it isn't fed what it wants when it is hungry, it will rampage and kill so many people."

"Why not shoot it? Put it down? Inject it with something?"

"You know we've tried. The thing is evil and lives only to hunt and eat humans. It's hide is stronger than even Kevlar, almost like there are protective scales beneath the fur. Nothing has worked. And until someone figures it out, it has to be this way. It is only tame when fed. We do it to save life."

2 REJECTION PROOF

Sandra cried while watching Ted from her prone position on the floor as he walked back into the kitchen. With one eye swollen shut and what felt like a broken rib, she found it hard to sit upright. She knew she had to escape. She knew the pain she felt was only the beginning. Or more precisely, the beginning of the end.

Grabbing the armrest of the easy chair, she pulled with her right arm. She used her left arm to hug the right side of her chest as if that act would help ease the pain. Pressing hard against herself for support, she could feel waves of agony radiating from it in proportional response to her movement. If a rib wasn't broken, it was damn sure bruised badly. With herculean effort she pulled herself up and stood. Her body convulsed in pain. Her head throbbed. Dizzy and disoriented, she made her way by memory from the living room towards the front door. Her vision was blurry in the one good eye with which she could still see. The one swollen shut created a problem with her depth perception. She had not dealt with that type of thing before.

Despite knowing the way, she bumped into an end table and a lamp. Knocking the lamp over, she heard the crash and sighed.

"Going somewhere?"

Sandra turned around to see Ted returning from the kitchen with a butcher knife. Seeing the twisted look of hatred on his face, she calmed down a little bit. She was beyond screaming and whimpering. She would not beg knowing there would be no mercy. Facing him, she forced herself to stand erect. He could see the swollen black eye. But he might not know about her broken rib. He might think she still had strength to fight. She was determined to present herself as formidable a foe as possible despite his advantages of height, weight, and strength.

She would act like the proverbial caged and trapped animal. He would be the zoo keeper keeping a wary eye upon her. That was the goal. If she could buy time, calm him down, talk him down, she might diffuse things. If not that, she might at least find a way to escape or a means to make the fight more equitable. It behooved her to remain calm and focused if she hoped to live. Her father had always taught her to be prepared and look for equalizers. She remembered this and scanned the room in hopes of finding a potential tool for such an occasion.

"I told you I was rejection proof." He said it with the utmost confidence while staring at her. "I've never lost a sale. I've never lost a woman. Never turned down on a date. I told you this. It will never happen. I am rejection proof. I control my own destiny."

"I know." She stalled for time by engaging him. "Why would I want to leave?" Her mind rattled off reasons in such rapid succession she couldn't keep count. But she dared not voice those thoughts and push Ted into a violent berserker rage. "I was just checking the door. I thought I heard something."

"No, you weren't. You want to leave. This much is obvious. We can't have that can we? It wouldn't be good for either of us now would it?"

"No, I guess not. I don't know what I was thinking about. I'm sorry."

She wasn't. But she was desperate. His hands dropped to his side as she spoke in soft tones without betraying any sense of fear. She would play to the hidden side of him. Somewhere, deep within this monster, was the caring and loving man she had known. If only she could reach that part of him, she would live long enough to get away forever.

"So, we are good? You understand your role?" He asked as he took a couple steps closer to her.

"Yes, honey. Why would I reject you? It was hormones. I need to see the doctor to get my meds worked out. It's not you. It's me."

As she stalled, she thought his demeanor was changing. But she also noticed something out of the corner of her eye on the couch and concocted a rudimentary plan of defense.

"Would you mind if I sat down? My head is starting to hurt?"

"Okay, let me help you over there."

"Oh, that's okay honey. I can do it. I want to sit down a minute."

Ted watched as Sandra moved towards the couch. She did her best to hide her chest pain by holding her head and drawing attention to that part of her body. "It hurts so bad." She said for extra effect.

"Would you like some aspirin?"

"Sure. Thanks."

As she sat down, she reached into the crochet bag on the couch and palmed one of her hooks while Ted walked back into the kitchen. She noticed he still had the knife in his hand. She decided to lean forward on the couch instead of leaning back. It would give her a better chance to launch into a run if needed. That position also allowed her to disguise the equalizer she now held.

Ted fumbled around in the kitchen opening cabinets until he found the aspirin in a drawer. After all this time he still didn't know where things went. She thought back to how his easy-going mannerisms changed as soon as they moved in together. Now she was in what felt like mortal danger. She should have seen the signs. Controlling. Angry mood swings. Isolating her from friends. Being blinded by love and the dream of a perfect relationship, she ignored the signs. She thought things would change and settle down. Now she was paying the price.

Walking back in, he noticed the position in which she was sitting. She was not leaning back and resting her head like she did when she had headaches before. She crouched like a tiger preparing to pounce on its prey.

"Bitch!" He yelled as he threw the aspirin aside and ran at her. Although startled, she still managed to jump up to her feet before he got there.

His right hand flew out and slapped her face hard. But she had prepared herself mentally for the blow. While it staggered her, it did not knock her down. She did not cry out.

He stood and stared. He looked stunned that she was still standing upright.

"That's enough of that shit." He yelled as he raised the knife above her head to come at her in a downward chopping motion.

She leapt forward with every last ounce of energy she had and raised her right arm. Screaming with the pain it caused, she thrust the crochet hook at his face and through his left eye.

Staggering a step, he fell to his knees reaching his hands up to pull it out of his face. Forcing herself forward, she put her weight behind the crochet hook and fell over on top of Ted as he died instantly.

Rolling to her left and onto her back, she reeled in pain and gasped for air. When the pain finally subsided enough to breathe without experiencing excruciating agony, she felt relief. She was safe. Finally. Turning her head to look at him, she wanted to make sure he was dead, to confirm it was over. This had to be the end for one of them – preferably him.

As she got up and grabbed her cell phone off the coffee table, she prepared to dial 911. She stopped and held the phone ready to hit 'dial.' All the while, she stared at him as if expecting the monster to rise from the dead and attack her.

She continued watching Ted for any remote resemblance of life. As her heartbeat slowed and adrenaline highs gave way to additional surges of pain, she made the call. As the phone rang, she found herself looking at and talking to Ted and realizing there is a first for everything. "Consider yourself rejected."

"911, What's your emergency?"

3 FLOWER CEREMONY

The traditions in the church were different than what I'd experienced elsewhere in my adult life. The flower ceremony was one of the many things we didn't experience elsewhere. Coming back to the Rock Lick Creek Church of the Brethren was always interesting no matter what the occasion. In the case of funerals, things seemed almost backwards here in this tiny family church in rural Kentucky. The church practiced according to the old ways. The pastor and the deacons held sway and controlled everything. And the congregation liked it that way. It was mandatory and ingrained in us to visit in support of major family events. And no matter how far away any of us got, we'd always see each other again at an event. We could leave the village and the church. But it never left us.

When Pastor Rollins finished with his benediction, none of us really felt better. The process of giving blessings and then opening up the parlor to view the deceased was something we knew growing up. But for those of us who came back, it felt odd. It didn't work that way 'out there' as the elders called the rest of the world. That phrase made me chuckle and think of how some Amish refer to everyone else as 'English' regardless of their nationality, language, or religion. It was Amish and it was English. That was it. Here in the church, it was the Brethren and 'out there.'

We walked in single file with the proper dignified and earnest demeanor into the parlor where the open casket of old man Bonnets lay in repose. The expectation was we would stop and kiss the old man on the forehead, say a prescribed prayer, and continue moving down the line where we would pick up wafers and a thumb-sized cup of wine for the communion which would follow. I got into the queue and did my duty as expected. Taking the communion items, I proceeded in a respectful and conscientious manner to take a seat and wait.

When everyone finished paying their respects and took their seats, the communion part of the service commenced. With the transubstantiation completed, and cups gathered, the deacons handed out hymnals. People held them. But no one opened them. The songs were rote. Ingrained in everyone's memories over a lifetime of repetition.

With no instruments allowed, the gathering sang in an a cappella chorus that made the early days of bad American Idol contestants seem glorious by comparison. The off-tune and non-harmonized singing went on for almost an hour. Many of us exchanged furtive glances in the parlor as we also looked at our phones to check the time. Those of us who had traveled to get here were ready to leave. Our duty was all but done, we knew only a few things remained before services could end. We wanted to get on with it and get back to our lives.

Pastor Rollins raised his hands and motioned for everyone to sit. We were getting close to the end of the service now. There were a few more prayers and words from the pastor. The deacons and elders walked solemnly up towards the coffin. As tradition dictated, they were bearing wreaths and flowers. As there was no male heir to perform it, the daughter and only child of old man Bonnets came forward for the flower ceremony. She kissed her father goodbye one last time. She slowly closed the lid upon the coffin and turned around to face the deacons which were standing spiritual guard. The pastor came over to hand her the largest wreath. The church purchased it for the occasion. They always had the largest wreath. While parishioners had to bring them, the church usually supplied them for a fee. The money raised would go to the next of kin.

Marisa Bonnets took and laid the large wreath upon the coffin over where her father's head would be. Stands were set up in advance for the placement of the other wreaths. The deacons and elders began to place them all around. We were close to the final benedictions and end of the service.

As the elders finished and took their seats, the pastor gave a large bouquet of flowers to Marisa and led her to the podium. With both of them facing the rest of us, the flower ceremony was going to take place.

Pastor Rollins smiled as he recited the good deeds of old man Bonnets and praised his daughter Marisa for vowing to keep the family farm running and support the church. She cried. We all knew that it was time to stand up. Marisa walked towards the rest of us a few paces then turned around 180 degrees. She dropped to her knees for the blessing. Anointing her forehead with oil, the pastor admonished her to hold true to her faith. She shook visibly. Shoulders heaving with heart-rending emotion. She nodded and we could hear her compose herself and say "Amen."

As she rose slowly from her kneeling position, she tossed the bouquet of flowers into the air behind her. When they hit me in the chest, I gasped. The ceremony ended. Next year the funeral would be for me.

4 NEW GLASSES

The visions started for me not long after my turn came to get upgraded lenses. On the day I got a new pair of glasses, I had a vastly improved ability to see and felt like a superhero. I thought I could see for miles and read with ease. It was amazing at first. But headaches followed hard on the heels of the euphoria. Mom, and then the optometrist, told me it was just a matter of my eyes adjusting. I knew that in general. My sister and I both experienced headaches when adjusting to new scripts. I had gone too long with the wrong one. The muscles in my eyes needed to relax and let the glasses make up for my visual shortcomings. I hated the headaches. But I loved having better eyesight. So, I stopped complaining even though the headaches didn't stop.

The used eye-wear program run by our local optometrist was a godsend to our family. The practice took donations and repurposed them for underserved socio-economic groups. It was our only source of new or gently used glasses. My sister and I both had a genetic predisposition requiring glasses. After our father died, getting updated prescriptions became difficult for our mother to handle. There wasn't enough money to go around. We didn't have any real expectations. One of us would get a new prescription. The other would wait until enough money was available. Sometimes the glasses were great. Sometimes, they made us feel ugly or uncomfortable. They often caused headaches as our eyes adjusted to a new pair. But our vision and our moods improved. Our confidence tended to soar when we were lucky enough to get a new pair with a proper prescription.

In the meantime, we struggled to read and learn. We got into fights. We got bullied. And we dreamed of escaping the situation once we were adults. We didn't blame mom. Times were hard and poverty hung over us like a black cloud.

I saw a pair that looked like the iconic John Lennon ones. That's what I wanted. He was my dad's hero. He listened to Lennon all the time whether it was The Beatles or John's solo work. The thought of being able to both see clearly and to look like Lennon was a double bonus. It was a visual reminder of my father. In this case, it was also beneficial that the previous owner had a head shaped like mine. The glasses fit. The script itself only needed minor tweaking of the lenses as the donor and I both had pretty bad vision. That fortunate set of circumstances made it easier on mom to afford to get mine updated.

The headaches never left. Nor did they diminish over the next couple of weeks. In conjunction with them, the visions came. They were like watching murder mysteries in small snippets. I'd have a bird's eye view of someone hit in the back of the head. My headache would spike in intensity. And then everything would return to normal. The visions were so realistic I could feel as well as see things happening. A claw hammer smashing into the back of someone's head would sink into the skull with a wet thump. I felt warm blood splattering on my face. Spraying blood coated my glasses. Instinctively, I even reached up to wipe them off.

I assumed these visions were a side-effect of the horrible migraines. While I'd never had visions before, I'd also never experienced quite as much pain before when adjusting to new glasses. The pain was so intense, I assumed it was something my brain did to cope and divert attention away from it. To my surprise and chagrin, the frequency and intensity of the visions increased while following no pattern I could discern. Lighting, time of day, activities, and other environmental factors would all be different. With nothing to tie them all together, there was no way to predict when it might occur or determine how to prevent or improve things.

I hesitated to tell mom about the visions. I thought if I told her about the visions, she'd take the glasses away. Then I'd be back to the previous norm which was unacceptable. I felt sure I could ride this out and adjust. My sister and I had ridden out the headaches before. I could do it now.

The diversity of the visions was like having a series of unrelated nightmares with a theme of violent deaths. I'd never seen so much blood as I did in these visions – not even in gory horror slasher movies. But then all would be gone again and the vision would dissipate. While they were happening, though, the violence taking place inside the visions was overwhelming and varied. While there would be stabbings, they would be different – from the front to the rear, in seeming self-defense, or in blatant attack. The blunt force attacks also differed. I remember with distinct clarity the claw hammer embedding into the back of someone's skull. It was the worst one. It was so realistic I obsessively kept trying to clean my glasses even after knowing it was just a vision and not real.

The hammer incident happened to be hands-down the worst and most violent one I remember. A close second was the time I could see a lady being repeatedly stabbed in the upper body and face. I could see the attacker's right arm swinging a large chef's knife into the woman. The stabbing motions happened with such rapidity I couldn't count the number of strokes. The sound of her screaming combined with the fear and pleading in her face were horrifying. The final sounds of her gurgling and choking on her own blood made me stagger.

I wondered if my subconscious mind was creating these visions out of some deep-seated anger or hidden motivation for revenge. The coupling of pain and violence worked in tandem. The more intense the pain, the more violent the vision. The scales ran in parallel. There was a direct correlation between them. Very mild headaches only seemed to stir up feelings of angst. Stronger ones pushed the feelings to a level of anger and hatred and became increasingly tied to miniature scenes of violence running through my mind like a horror movie trailer.

Despite the reassurances of mom and the doctor, the headaches did not go away. My eye muscles did not appear to adjust to the new script as quickly as they should have. On top of that, the frequency of the visions increased. Nevertheless, I remained determined not to say anything about the visions. Not only did I fear losing the new glasses, but I also feared everyone would think I was crazy. I watched scores of people get attacked and killed. The visions and migraines had become so intense that the pain left me convulsing.

Many times, I would find myself on the floor balled up in a fetal position. Often I found myself shaking. I did my best to keep all of this stuff a secret. After all, I had superhero vision now. I could overcome the hurdles. There was no going back now.

Despite my best efforts to hide things, mom walked into the den one day when I was convulsing on the floor. She thought I had a seizure when she saw it happen. She rushed me to the ER. I was in so much pain, I did not protest. I felt like the jig was up and I'd be losing my new glasses as soon as the truth came out.

Blood tests and scans came back negative in quick succession. They ordered more tests. It was a long day. I spent time in between tests recounting my experiences. I explained everything to my mother. As she was scolding me for keeping the visions a secret and hiding the intensity of the headaches, a charge nurse came into the room to prepare me for more tests. I collapsed from a sitting position in my hospital bed and started convulsing. Upon seeing me rocking in rhythmic contractions and screaming in pain, the nurse quickly took off my glasses to keep me from breaking them. Almost immediately I stopped shaking.

The nurse turned on the TV in the room. It provided some background noise while she asked more questions of my mother and me. I paid little attention. I wanted to relax. I felt like I'd pass out from exhaustion.

As the questioning continued I only interjected information occasionally. Local news played in the background. Before I dozed off, I saw the headlines and the reporters discussing a break in a case.

A serial killer had been captured. He had gotten himself into a car accident in a police chase. His finger prints matched those on file from several murders. As a photo of his blurry face came on the screen, I squinted and thought I saw him wearing the same type of John Lennon style glasses I had chosen. His official mug shot was not very clear. But in it, I could tell that he wasn't wearing glasses. They played a cell phone video from someone who saw the accident and started recording things. The suspect was screaming and cursing as he was being led cuffed from his wrecked car to the back of a police cruiser. For the parts the television station didn't bleep out, he was yelling that if he hadn't lost his glasses a few weeks ago, he would still be free.

When I awakened, my glasses were sitting on the rolling table next to my bed. When I grabbed them, I looked at mom with confusion. They were my old glasses with the wrong script. Looking back, she nodded to me letting me know I needed to put them on my head.

"We'll get the script changed on these."

I wanted to know what happened to my Lennon-esque frames. But I didn't need to ask.

"After we made the connection between your migraines & visions to those cursed glasses, we got rid of them. The police have them now as potential evidence in their investigation."

5 CABIN GETAWAY

Surrounded by snow laden pines high on the slopes of Poor Mountain, the cabin was chosen as an idyllic winter retreat for Rosalie and her friends. It promised to provide the getaway that they needed from their hectic lives.

The log cabin creaked and moaned with the wind and weight of the snow upon its roof even as the crackling of the fire added a harmonious voice to the serenade. The smell of pine filled the air. Shadows from the flames danced about playfully as they cozied up to the warmth of the stone fireplace.

Relaxing and putting the world behind them, they were laughing, drinking wine, and sharing stories. Rosalie was especially excited about the trip. It was a chance to unwind after a horrible divorce finally ended a violent and verbally abusive marriage. She had jumped at the idea when her friend Jan first mentioned the possibility of a post-divorce getaway.

Revelry and laughter progressed as the friends unwound and relaxed until Laura suggested they tell some ghost stories.

Mia balked. She didn't want to upset Rosalie after all she'd been through. Her years with Kevin had been horrible and scary enough.

"That's not appropriate."

"It's okay. It could be fun. I mean these are ghost stories, not Kevin stories. I'm safe from that asshole and we're isolated in this cabin. What better time and place to tell ghost stories? Night. Snow and wind. Crackling fire. All y'all gathered around with me. Let's do it."

Rosalie's response brought a smile to everyone.

Tales of the Snarly Yow started things off. They were followed up by tales of Banshees and wailing ghosts as if to coincide with the increase in the howling wind. The tales went on for several hours as the snow blanketed their cars.

"This is perfect." Katie said as she poured herself another glass of wine.

"Just what I needed. Harmless fun. Laughing and telling impossible stories with my dearest friends after all the crap I've been through. I love y'all. You've been here for me every step of the way." Rosalie raised her glass to toast her friends.

They continued their stories while the snow continued to fall. Their tales covered the cryptids, ghosts, aliens, and urban legends of the Appalachians totally unaware of the lore surrounding Poor Mountain itself.

When the snow stopped and the wind died down with it, the only sounds in the cabin came from their talking and the crackling of the fire they were cozied up around. Noticing the sudden lack of noise, Katie suggested they go outside and take a look at the landscape under a bright moon and the stars visible from this slope.

"You can't see stars where we live. Let's check things out. The views in the mountain in this bright moonlight must be pretty awesome." She walked to the door expecting her friends to follow her.

They left the cabin together to explore the surrounding woods under the silvery moon and starlight. As they strolled the splendid wintery landscape, the forest echoed with their laughter until a guttural bone-chilling growl cut through the air sending shivers down their spines. It seemingly rumbled through the pines and all other forest sounds stopped. Not a bird could be heard. Even the creaking of tree branches heavy with the weight of snow seemed to stop. The noise sent a shiver down their spines.

"What the fuck was that?" Jan asked as her eyes darted about looking for the source of the sound.

"Probably just the wind." Mia tried to sound reassuring even though her heart also raced. Inside, she felt that something was incredibly wrong.

They panicked as they heard a gunshot and a large figure started emerging from the trees. Terror had replaced laughter and smiles.

"Run!" They all seemed to shout in unison as they headed back for the cabin.

Rosalie's heart pounded as she ran to the sanctuary of their retreat. Glancing back, she saw the figure advancing on them. She couldn't make out what it was. The figure was obscured in shadow and snow that started falling and blowing off branches as the wind picked back up.

Entering the lodge, they closed and locked the door. Almost immediately, a loud thump shook the cabin door. The friends jumped in fear from the startling noise.

"It's trying to break the door down. Did you hear that?"

"Of course we heard it Jan. What the fuck? We're all standing right here. What should we do?" Mia responded with a voice punctuated by fear and anger.

The thump came again as the cabin door was hit. It was louder and more violent than the last time.

"Quick, help me push this couch over against the door." Rosalie commanded.

As they pushed it over, they heard what sounded like a scuffle outside the cabin. Then another gunshot.

"Are there two of them? What the hell could they want from us? What are they shooting at? WTF is happening?" Katie was hysterically rubbing her hands together and glancing all around the cabin as if she couldn't focus.

Jan went to try to look out the window. "I can't see anything. The snow is swirling around in the wind too much and the door is at a weird angle from this window."

The noises outside seemed to grow louder and seemed accompanied by growling sounds that raised goosebumps on them.

Another sound like a gunshot rang out. Then the door seemed to bow inward a little bit with the weight and ferocity of a renewed thump.

"I know you're in there Rosalie. Make this easy on yourself and open the damn door. If I have to break it down, I'm going to kill all of you."

"Kevin?" Rosalie asked softly and lowly enough where only her friends could hear the whispered question.

"GO AWAY KEVIN!" Mia faced the door and took charge of the situation. "WE HAVE WEAPONS!"

More calmly, she turned to look at her friends. "Everyone grab something. Knife. Candlestick holder. Fire poker. Whatever you might be able to use as a weapon. This asshole is not getting to Rosalie. Not while I have breath."

They all walked around in the cabin picking up things they thought might be useful. The door thumped again.

"I warned you. I already shot your damn dog twice. There's nothing left but this door between us. I will get through it."

"Dog?" Several of them looked at each other with perplexed expressions. None of them had a dog.

"Maybe there was a feral dog or wolf or coyote out there. Maybe that was the source of the scuffle noises – not two people. Kevin and a wolf." Rosalie tried to reason.

"Coyotes don't come up here. They prefer the lower pasture areas where there are more food sources than up here on heavily forested peaks. And I don't think we have wolves in Virginia." Mia said.

Another thump on the door. "This is getting old Rosalie. You're seriously pissing me off. We can continue to do this the hard way or you can make it easier and spare your friends some pain."

"None of this makes sense. How did he know where we were or even that we were going on a little getaway in the first place? What's the dog he's talking about?" Jan asked.

"Maybe it's the Snarly Yow." Mia said in an ill-fated attempt at humor. As her friends scowled at her, she apologized. "Just trying to ease some tension here. Sorry."

Another thump shook the door even as howling could be heard.

"Your damn dog is resilient. But this time I'll make sure it gets a bullet in its head. Then it's your turn."

Kevin's comment was followed by an eerie silence. Only occasional guttural howls could be heard.

"What's happening out there?" Rosalie asked as she walked towards a window to try to peer out. Something huge passed by the window. "Something's out there. And it's big."

"A bear?" Mia asked. "Maybe it wasn't a dog but a bear that Kevin saw."

"Maybe. It was big. And they are pretty sturdy – even when shot." Jan replied. "But they are not typically aggressive. They're not polar bears or grizzlies. These black bears are pretty shy and tend to walk away from humans."

"I don't know. But it was big. I couldn't get a view of it with the frosted windows and snow swirling about." Rosalie tried to put together in her mind what she had seen but couldn't quite figure it out.

Two shots rang out in rapid succession. Then the door thumped louder than it had previously.

The ladies instinctively retreated away from the door and towards the fireplace. During all the commotion, they had left the fire unattended. They did not have much more than glowing embers at this point and suddenly noticed they were all getting ice cold. And fresh firewood was stacked in a shed outside.

The door had nearly buckled inward.

"Last call for alcohol."

"Fuck him." Mia said with renewed determination even through chattering teeth.

Beneath winters icy grip, each renewed assault on the cabin became stronger and louder. The door was beginning to buckle. Their sanctuary was becoming a frost tomb.

The women huddled together with their makeshift weapons. With their backs to the fireplace, they faced the cabin door and waited for the inevitable. Their hearts raced. Their shallow breaths, each fraught with a combination of fear and resolve, were visible in the frigid air inside the cabin.

With a deafening crash, the door splintered and burst open with shards of wood flying into the cabin. Kevin lunged inside. But he wasn't alone.

The women screamed and raised their weapons defiantly as Kevin went flying through the air in their direction. He landed a couple feet from them. In terror, they saw blood all over his body.

Behind him a large figure advanced. It's face was obscured by frost and its body a seeming whirlwind of snow. It roared so loudly Katie dropped her fire shard and covered her ears.

Rosalie advanced to swing a skillet at the beast. Even hitting it squarely on the side of the head with all the might she could muster didn't knock it down.

The thing roared again in defiance even though it was momentarily disoriented by the blow. This gave them precious seconds to brace for battle. The monster advanced towards them. In the vortex of swirling snow that hung upon it, a hairy paw reached out and down. It grabbed Kevin by the back of his shirt and batted him effortlessly into the air where it caught his arm in his massive jaws.

Holding him in the air and staring at him, the beast shook Kevin like a dog with a chew toy. They weren't sure if it was playing with its prey or making sure it was dead.

"Run!" Rosalie yelled.

Taking advantage of the distraction of the beast, they all ran through the opening created by the shattered cabin door.

As they ran, they could hear howling behind them. "Don't look back. Run!" Mia said.

Tripping and stumbling in the snow and forest, they did their best to run down the gravel road leading up to the cabin when they saw headlights coming up the mountain.

They stopped. Behind them the howling continued. Before them, a car approached. Waving their hands frantically, they tried to get the attention of the driver.

As the vehicle got closer, it stopped. A young man got out of the truck with a rifle in his hands.

"What's going on here?"

The ladies looked back at the cabin and pointed. "Snow monster? Bear? We don't know." Rosalie said. "My husband is dead."

"Ex. Fucking ex-husband bastard who tried to get in and kill us all." Katie said.

"Where is he?" The man asked.

As they all looked back at the cabin, the vortex of snow walked out of the cabin dragging Kevin's corpse through the snow behind it.

"There. The thing killed him." Jan said.

The man put his rifle back into the truck.

"Aren't you going to shoot it?" Mia asked.

"Shoot what? You can't kill Poor Mountain. This entity is older than humankind. Even the natives who preceded us. This essence of the mountain takes different forms depending on the season. It doesn't wander into towns

32

or farms. It stays up here. It protects the mountain and it's denizens. Shooting at it would only make it come after us."

"Kevin shot at it. Many times. He thought it was a dog we had up here with us." Rosalie responded.

"Not a dog. Not a bear. It is Poor Mountain itself. And if Kevin shot at it, he made a mistake."

"If you want a ride, I can take you somewhere for you to spend the night. There are other cabins in the area and a couple of hiking shelters not too far away."

"What about Kevin?" Rosalie asked.

"What about him? Fuck him. He deserved what he got." Mia replied.

"But his body?"

"He belongs to Poor Mountain now. You'll never find his body." The man said.

Looking back at the cabin and pondering their situation, they tried to get a glimpse of the beast. It had disappeared into the trees dragging Kevin with it.

"Yeah. Take us somewhere. With that door broken down we'd freeze up here. We can worry about cars tomorrow in the daylight." Jan said. The others nodded in agreement as they piled into the truck.

They had set out on a trip to escape the hectic lives and stressors they faced. In turn, they faced a new and unknown darkness. And in that remote cabin, they reinforced an unbreakable bond and learned a new ghost tale for future outings.

6 THE FISHERMAN

The last time he pulled his boat into the harbor, a crowd gathered to watch the spectacle. What he had in his net was so bizarre and unexpected that people still talked about it in whispers and crossed themselves for protection when they did. As a kid, I thought it was something akin to a magic trick. It had to be since there were no such things as mermaids.

I could not press through the crowd to see up close. But I was able to find a great vantage point atop Old Man Murphy's pub. It sat elevated above the port and the sloping thatch roof gave me a great bird's eye view of the harbor as the Fisherman docked at a wooden pier.

Mermaid or not, we all saw *something*. I thought I saw a woman with flowing red hair squirming around in a giant fishing net as the Fisherman fully lowered it with a pulley. But the press of the crowd and the arrival of the police ended up blocking my view. I never saw exactly what they pulled out of the net once it was lowered.

He disappeared after that day. At least, he disappeared from our little coastal town of Portkilly. As rare as his appearances had been in the past, they were non-existent these days. In the pubs, people said that modern fishing methods, high-tech equipment, and changes in faith and spirituality altered his craft making it nearly archaic. I was an ignorant teenager when he lowered the redhaired wonder from his deck. Hell, I'm ignorant of his ways now.

Rumors and legends abounded. He always caught what he set out to catch. Shark, giant octopus, and, well, even mermaids were no match for him. People joked that the reason there were no Kraken anymore was because Queen Victoria hired him to catch them all. Of course, the absurdity of such legends and longevity were embellished and exaggerated for effect. They took on outlandish and impossible proportions.

Looking back, I found myself a bit surprised that he was still alive. He seemed old to me then. But I never was a good judge of age.

I searched across many towns and pubs following rumors of his appearance somewhere along the coast. When I accidentally and surprisingly ran across him in a pub, I was stunned. I didn't believe it was really the Fisherman. So, I asked a lot of questions while trying to ascertain if it was him. Is it really you? I had to know. What I had seen and heard that day so long ago was fresh in my mind some twenty-five years later.

He drank his whiskey without a word. He nodded from time to time as if any question were answerable with a yes or a no. For the price of a couple of shots, he finally agreed to speak to me. He confirmed he was the Fisherman. A lifetime seemed to have come and gone since I had seen him lower his net onto a pier in Portkilly. Things had changed for both of us.

He had kept to himself, skirting the Atlantic Coast of Western Ireland. He'd sell fish to make a meager living, feed himself, and pay for drink and docking fees. But he hadn't taken a commission since that day. When the local authorities and Gardaí had all but flogged him and Father O'Bannon threatened to excommunicate him, he had gone away with no intention of plying his trade that way again.

He lamented that he had given up the trade. He said it helped people even though they frowned upon his activities. Having come to some of my own conclusions over the years, I asked more questions.

He confirmed it was not a mermaid I saw that day. He had pulled a woman from the sea. Her nakedness created such a stir that all kinds of accusations swirled about him. The growing threats and hatred had driven him away. He swore to me he had never touched her. He had only retrieved her from the sea.

I called for another shot for the Fisherman. I asked if he would be willing to take a commissioned job from me.

He threw back that shot in one gulp and asked for another. It followed the other in a similar manner. He raised the brim of his Donegal Tweed and cast a wary eye upon me. The shadows in the pub obscured most of his haggard sea-worn face. Aged with wrinkles and salt water, his eye stared at me with an intensity I had never seen in another person.

He whispered that there was no guarantee that he could do it. He was out of practice. Many years had passed.

I acknowledged his comments with a nod, and we walked out of the pub. Although she'd died in a car accident ten years earlier when a dumb American tourist hit her head-on while driving on the wrong side of the road, I had a chance. I could well hold my own mermaid once again. The Fisherman would try to retrieve her from the sea of death. With any luck, her flowing auburn hair would soon cascade over her shoulders in his net as he lowered her from the deck of his boat and into my waiting embrace.

7 SAYING GOODBYE

When it comes down to it, I never got the hang of saying goodbye to someone who was dying or who had already died. Somehow, closure seemed to elude me and I found the whole process absurd and tiresome.

My therapist, my family, and even my friends told me more often than I cared to hear that I needed to get closure when someone died. Thinking back, I assume there was a level of dissociation wrapped around denial that kept me from doing the things they did – or which they expected me to do.

If I admitted that the person was gone, where would that leave me? It sounds stupid in retrospect. Life goes on and people adjust to newfound gaps in their lives most of the time. I have seen many instances where lifelong partners never recovered from the death of a spouse of many decades. Instead, they would themselves die shortly thereafter as if willing themselves to go walk beyond the veil of life and death and regain the intimacy of the relationship they lost.

It wasn't the same for friends or even parents' deaths. The pain was real enough and the losses felt in the marrow of the bones. But it was not the same kind of loss, if indeed there is such a thing as the categorization of deaths.

Yet there I was sitting in the car trying to figure out how to say goodbye to a long-term friend. The funeral would be taking place soon and to say I felt shocked at the sudden death would be an understatement. I was in no way prepared for this to have happened. I had no idea how I was even going to try to say goodbye and get some closure.

With the car parked on the one-way street which wound its way through the cemetery, I wondered how I would go about saying farewell to my friend. I didn't know what to say or how to say it. I felt like something needed to happen. All those years of chiding from friends and family took a toll and weighed upon me. I needed to figure out something and I needed to do it soon.

But I could not figure out for the life of me what to do or say. So, I sat and watched the funeral from inside the relative safety of the car. No one would pay attention to me and I could work it out in my mind.

Although I tried, I could not watch everything as people milled about and got into smaller groups blocking the view from time to time. But I saw enough. Reality broke through my barriers. I began to feel hot tears pouring down my cheeks while weird feelings of loss grew in my heart. It added to my confusion and indecision. I'd never quite felt this way before and didn't know how to process what was going on within me.

Almost everyone who showed up was wearing black, walking slowly, talking in quiet whispers, nodding their heads at others. It was quite surreal. I tried to force myself to open the door and get out and partake in the mourning and the ritual send off. But I couldn't move. I was stuck in a place of indecision, fear, pain, and other things I don't know how to describe in an adequate manner.

The ceremony seemed lovely and the people appeared to be experiencing genuine grief at the loss. Yet, they also seemed to find comfort in each other while sharing memories. As everyone made their way back to their cars, I couldn't help but chastise myself for not getting out and partaking.

As everyone left the graveyard, the procession of cars meandered through the rolling hills at a very slow pace. There wasn't any need for a police escort for this part. They had long since left. No one had their lights on anymore. It was just a matter of everyone making their way to the memorial luncheon.

I never got the hang of those post burial meals either. I wasn't sure I wanted to take part in this one. They seemed awkward. There was something odd about it to me. You bury someone you love and then go laugh and eat and carry on with each other. Something made me process that as disingenuous. Here was a group of people gathered together seemingly in unity. But most of them I hadn't seen in ages. All these luncheons were like that – at least in my experience. People came out of the woodwork as if virtue signaling that they loved and cared for the deceased whether it was true or not. While I did not like it, it seemed to be an established ritual and helped people to mourn together. I always hated it and felt uncomfortable at such events. I would try to find a reason to excuse myself, give my condolences, and leave post haste.

When we pulled into the parking lot of this large Italian restaurant, I had made up my mind I was not going to go in and immerse myself in this one either. Even though I love Italian food, I wouldn't partake. Pasta was always a comfort food to me and my emotional state would otherwise drive me to indulge. But I would forgo festivities. My friend and I would meet up for dinner at this very restaurant once a month. But in this scenario and setting I wasn't hungry. The circumstances for enjoying the food at this place were minimal at best. I couldn't break bread with my friend ever again. Those days were over. We'd never laugh and reminisce about our adventures. The finality of it was overwhelming. The future was set and that was all relegated to memories now. Sadness overwhelmed me. I needed to sit this one out.

With the decision made, I put my hand on my friend's shoulder and told him I would miss him but it was time for me to go. He shivered and turned to look as if he'd heard and felt something. But he hadn't seen me before and didn't see me now as I was fading away and drifting out of the car. I needed to join my body and follow the natural sequence of things. I could hear the dirt hitting the top of the coffin back at the cemetery. It was calling out to me.

8 THE WASTING

When the first symptoms appeared, it became obvious that this was not the normal seasonal flu. The media hyped the possibility of a leaked experimental virus more devastating and quicker acting than even COVID-19 was. It presented itself initially like a mild flu. People experienced dry coughs, headaches, body aches, general body soreness, and fevers. Accompanying these symptoms was a general feeling of malaise. While people went to doctors for help and treatment of flu symptoms, their bodies began to change.

The skin of those infected became sallow. Depending on the person's normal pigmentation, the color of their skin became either yellowish-brown or an ashen-gray color. Their eyes seemed to sink into their sockets. Light sensitivity increased to the point of people wearing sunglasses in the evening. Doctors could not pinpoint anything with tests. Researchers had no luck in isolating anything. They had even less of a chance to come up with a solution or preventative measures.

I wasn't sure what to think of this new thing. Every year there was a new scare of some dire disease or event that was going to wipe out humanity. I heard so many prognostications over the years I tended to take them in stride. The world never collapsed into a dark age. There was no Thanos-like event where half the world's population died at the snap of a finger. No meteor came. No missiles triggered a nuclear winter. I'd lived through so many such things that this just seemed like one more to add to the list.

At least until I got it.

I isolated myself in my basement. I was already somewhat light sensitive before getting this disease. As there was no treatment available, I tried to ride it out. My fever seemed to stay around 102 despite how many OTC acetaminophen tablets I took. My other symptoms increased. My skin became scaly and I had the look of someone who had recently undergone radiation therapy. It had those honeycomb type marks on it. Taking on an ashen grey color myself, I began to think I looked like an old alligator-human hybrid. I started having nightmares and weird day visions when I'd pass out. I'd wake up shivering and sweating despite also feeling cold and dehydrated.

I watched the television nonstop. I noticed that many hospitals were experiencing an overflow of people coming for treatments that didn't exist and refusing to leave. They gathered in hallways and anywhere there was room to find a seat on the floor. Reports focused on the problem and hospital administrators demanded authorities act. Meanwhile, things were happening in the background they weren't talking about, at least not in detail.

People packed in rooms and hallways like a container of sardines were dying. At first it was hard to tell just watching the videos. With people packed in and leaning against each other, the press of the crowd held them in place until someone moved. But when people did move or try to stand up, I started noticing that others would collapse from a sitting position as if their body had snapped in half. The torso would fall to one side at an almost 90-degree angle from the hips and lower body which remained in place on the floor.

News reports lamented the overcrowding and unbearable situation. They talked about the unsanitary conditions and people dying in the halls. But they didn't mention the way the bodies seemed somehow detached as if there was no spine or musculoskeletal system.

I stared at these reports mesmerized. I spent a lot of time researching things online looking for some potential explanation. Social media conspiracy theorists posited a dozen different scenarios with claims which mostly ranged from governmental experiments to an attack by a foreign enemy, focusing on the usual suspects of North Korea, Russia, China, and Iran. I never found anything online that really made sense and wasn't going to go down any of the rabbit holes of conspiracy.

So, during the reports I got to a place where I ignored the talking on the TV and tried to focus my attention as best I could on the scenes behind the reporters. It wasn't until one of those late-night paranormal shows came on that I realized something more was going on than a weird flu. One of the newer ghost & monster hunter type shows said they'd received reports of ghosts haunting the basement of a remote hospital.

It was so overrun by people the staff had left and the hospital ceased operations while waiting for authorities to clear everyone out and restore order. But the people remained in a growing sense of mass hysteria and confusion demanding treatment. The show played a teaser saying they had obtained footage from this hospital and evidence of ghosts.

As I grew more tired even from sitting around, I watched with anticipation. It started out with all the typical stuff these shows do. They walked you through their set up, their test methods, their theories, the stories they'd heard, and what they expected to find. For an hour-long show, 45 minutes of it was discussing their set-up and how they were going to capture proof of any paranormal activity in the hospital. Twelve minutes of it was commercial breaks. But those other three minutes were worth the hour of my time. It only took three minutes to realize this was bigger than anyone knew. Those three minutes before the end of the show and the final commercials was something altogether different.

Paralyzed with fear at what I saw, I was unable to move. The ghostly figures they came across while filming were the same ones from my recent dreams. Although they weren't ghosts. I had thought in my feverish sleep that I was having nightmares. I wrote them off as symptoms of this whole thing. I had nightmares during previous high fever sicknesses or when taking certain pain medications. So, I tended to pay little attention to them.

But here they were on TV. My visions. My nightmares. They were there for all to see. They captured them on night-vision cameras with their specialized infrared filters. I usually considered these tricks of light and photography. Fun to watch but not real.

Yet here I lay in bed watching the screen as I see an alien figure walking down a corridor towards the cameramen. The contorted face seemed twisted in an otherworldly smile. The grotesque nature of it was exactly like my dreams had been.

As it walked in the corridor, it would reach out a fingerless appendage and touch random people on the head. If they were not propped into place by others, they would fall over as if they snapped in half. It moved with slow determination. The cameramen themselves did not see it. The commentary was later added in closed captions on the screen after the fact and before airing. Their closed-caption comments revealed the startling effects their IR cameras produced.

The alien touched several people as it moved down the hall. It walked past the cameramen and out of view while the ghost hunters continued to film and talk. Their talk turned to coming back at another time to try a few more things but they admitted they had not seen anything on this trip. They built up the hype about ghosts only revealing themselves under certain circumstances and at certain times. Their timing was off. They'd be back and keep coming back until they could prove the existence of ghosts or disprove and give up trying to get a sighting from this place.

I fell asleep terrified at what I had seen. When I awoke at a start, I immediately wondered if I'd actually been asleep dreaming about seeing what I thought I saw on that show. The fever was still the same and it made sense to me that my day visions and nightmares were messing with me.

I looked up at the television. The news ran in the background. They were calling this new disease 'The Wasting.' They started talking about how people were wasting away and their skeletons becoming mushy and pliable inside them. The Center for Disease Control (CDC) and the World Health

Organization (WHO) were calling for people to immediately get more light, especially sun light if possible. Somehow light would counter the effects of this 'wasting.'

But people were not interested. Beset with extreme light sensitivity, many refused to follow the prescribed course of action. Combined with malaise, fevers, and other symptoms, many others were unable to comply.

Then I looked up and saw it again. This sickly green colored thing came towards me. This alien reached out it fingerless appendage as if pointing towards me, as if indicating it was my turn.

I didn't have much energy. I couldn't hope to fight. I couldn't run. I could barely move. I had too many body aches and pains holding me down. I had become frail and emaciated from the lack of food. I was wasting away physically and mentally. I was nothing like the person I'd been mere weeks before.

While feeling helpless, I had enough energy to talk.

"Lights on."

I shielded my eyes from the light as best I could. I held a hand above my brow pressed against my forehead to block out the overhead lights. Sunglasses were already on my face. And I watched through squinted eyes as the alien figure withdrew its arm. It was menacing looking; but it stood still. It was leaning in my direction but not moving. Then it started to fade from view.

Then it was gone as quickly as it had appeared. I continued to listen to the news in the background. But I closed my eyes half from fear and half from the pain of the light. I pulled a sheet over my head and fell back asleep despite my fear. Exhaustion, the fever, and the continuing pain overwhelmed me. I could not force myself to stay awake and alert.

From the moment I awakened, the alien disease which was consuming me started to improve in dramatic fashion. It dissipated as fast as it had come over me. I had enough energy to go upstairs and open curtains.

Allowing more light into the house seemed to improve my strength and mood.

In the background, news reports were covering the successful use of light around the world to combat the effects of the 'wasting' disease. I began to notice that no mention of aliens was ever made. I wondered how many people had seen what I had seen. I wondered if I'd seen anything at all or if it was just hallucinations. And I wondered about the odd imprints on the rug in my basement.

9 STARTING OVER

It did not begin as total madness that day. But Mondays were prone to be bad days for Dave Raspey. This one was to prove no exception to that rule. Everyone had their 'Mondays suck' stories. Social media was full of memes. There were songs about Mondays. They were also the worst day of the week for Dave. Getting started with a fresh week was bad enough. Having a series of mandatory meetings every Monday as well as quotas for calls didn't help. He had to do so much, he dreaded it every week. Often the Monday blues would start midday on Sunday.

He tried to get the endorphins flowing in preparation for the dreaded day. At least he could change the hormone balance in his system. It would help fight the overwhelming pressure he felt every Monday when he awoke. So, he laid out his jogging clothes on Sunday night. That way they were staring him in the face in the morning. He had made it into a habit of getting out and running. It might be jogging or fast walking some of the time, but the main thing was he'd be moving. Blood would be circulating. Heart pumping. Endorphins flowing. This Monday was no different. He dressed and went out for a run. When he got back from the run, he tossed his rain-dampened ski-cap into the nearest chair. Then he ran his fingers through his thinning hair.

"Shelley?" He called out to his wife.

She appeared at the bedroom door in a slinky negligee and moved to hug him. He buried his face in her thick auburn hair and kissed her neck.

"Take a short loving embrace stud muffin." She invited him.

He tightened his embrace and grabbed her like an animal.

"Caveman need." He said in his best Neanderthal voice.

"That's enough." She said and pushed him back. "Go take a shower already. You smell like the missing link!"

He chuckled and shuffled off to take a shower and get dressed for work. No loving this morning, he thought. Although she hadn't called him stud muffin in years. He wondered what had brought that on this morning. Not that he was complaining. This morning might not pan out for him. But he'd be thinking about things all day long. He hoped this would not be another regular Monday from hell for him.

As he prepared to shove off to work, Shelley grabbed him and gave him a very passionate kiss.

"Hurry back tonight baby. I've got a surprise for my stud muffin."

"I can't wait!"

Images of her nude body ran through his head. It was going to be a long day watching the clock tick as he fantasized about what the evening might bring to him. This morning had started off well and the night would end better. *Best. Monday. Ever.* He thought. That's a nice change of pace.

He rushed down the block to catch the waiting bus. As he got on and found a seat, he kept mentally running through the morning in his head. '*She called me stud muffin again; and talked of a surprise*' he mumbled to himself. He thought something strange was going on. Why complain? At least he would be getting some TLC tonight. But she was acting like a teenager, like when they first got married. It hadn't been that way in years.

He couldn't help but concentrate on that thought. He was overthinking again. He needed to push the weird thoughts out of his head. He needed to forget the whys, the ifs, and the buts. He wanted to forget all the things running through his head and concentrate on the positive. She wanted him to hurry home. She had a surprise. She called him stud muffin. She kissed him with passion. *Turn off those stupid soundtracks.* He reprimanded himself mentally. *Accentuate the positive.* He repeated the mantra he couldn't quite place. *Who was it that said that? Johnny Mercer? Bing Crosby?* Mom played it on vinyl all the time. *Ugh. Stop with all the random thoughts. Concentrate.* He could hardly wait to get back home after work. The anticipation was building up in him and he still had an 8-hour day of work in front of him. He managed to turn down the dial on the soundtracks playing in his mind. He worked hard at his job all day. He did his best to push away any stray thoughts about the night awaiting him.

At the Stuart Advertising Agency, it was business as usual at first. During the day, he had made several new contacts for prospective accounts. He was doing very well on his quota for calls that day despite spending a few hours in meetings. By the end of the day though he had lost 2 accounts. The Hall Food Corp executives said that they didn't even remember him. Maybe they hadn't liked his ideas. Who knows? But old Mr. Stuart had somehow heard about it. Upset was an apt description of his feelings.

The president of Warren Paper Products had also called up old Mr. Stuart himself to complain. He said that nobody ever showed up on their scheduled video chat. He did not get a proposed layout for their upcoming series of commercials. Dave remembered giving the presentation. He knew what Mr. Warren was wearing. His signature flag bowtie. He couldn't understand why Mr. Warren would say such a thing. The video call had not been contentious in any way. Maybe he hadn't liked his ideas either. But saying he hadn't shown up was a bit extreme. They were on the video call for at least 45 minutes – 15 minutes longer than the allotted time. If he was going to complain, he should have complained that it took too long. Longer than he agreed to spend on the meeting and not that it never even took place.

About the middle of the afternoon, Mr. Stuart questioned him about the new contacts. He provided his report which was in meticulous notes. They were also entered into the company's proprietary CRM. Mr. Stuart took his notes and went to his own office to make follow-up calls that afternoon. When he did, it turned out that nobody knew of Dave Raspey. He did not show up anywhere in anyone's recollections. If Dave had made the calls as he indicated in the CRM, some of these clients would have remembered him. Some might forget. It's the nature of cold calls. People will give you the brush off. They get so many calls some days they have no idea who called them. It's all canned responses. *I'm busy. Can't talk now. Gotta go into a meeting. Try me next week. I'm happy with my current partners and suppliers. We don't have a budget.* The objections were nothing new and were part and parcel of the job at hand. Mr. Stuart knew that. Dave knew it too. Falsifying attempted call logs was not his style. Nor was entering fake data into the CRM. Neither action was acceptable.

Mr. Stuart called Dave into his office to discuss his findings. It was nothing new. The old man did this to everyone. He went in intervals. It could be daily for a week, or it could be once a quarter. But the old man double checked and micro-managed everyone's work to some extent. It wasn't anything new to Dave. And he knew he'd done his work. It was his turn to hear the old man's lecture. To listen to the obligatory *'you did okay but I need you to work harder'* speech. Then he'd be that much closer to getting home for his surprise.

He entered Mr. Stuart's office and took the seat across from the old man's desk. Mr. Stuart kept a huge Victorian hand-carved oak desk in the room so it would seem imposing. The tall, deep, cushioned chair facing it often made people feel confined. That added to the discomfort. That's the way the old man liked it. He was in charge and he wanted everyone to know it. Dave was familiar with the setup. Only new employees got alarmed when called into the office. Others got used to it after a few times.

"I'm sorry Dave," Mr. Stuart started, "but I'm going to have to let you go. You're not putting forth any quality work."

Dave sat stunned. He objected. He once again showed his call logs to Mr. Stuart by pointing to the report on the boss's desk. He also reminded him that all notations were in the company's CRM system. While he hated it, that proprietary CRM system had also saved his hide more than once. Despite the pain of doing all that data entry, it served to cover him many times. He could document every call and every email down to the minute of the day that it occurred. Mr. Stuart nodded his head. He believed the customers' reports and not the data in front of him. He insinuated that Dave had made false entries instead of actually doing any work. It was inexcusable.

"I've called most of the people on this list Dave. You must have known that I would do follow-ups when I took the list from you. No one knew who you were. No one recollected receiving a call from you. In short, these logs are lies. I don't know why you would fake the work. Even if everyone slammed the phone down on you and refused to talk to you, someone would have remembered a call. It would be their chance to complain and demand removal from our call lists. There were none. You might as well have not even existed."

He didn't understand. It was like a conspiracy. He couldn't figure out why a group of total strangers would conspire against him. Dave was at a loss. He knew he'd made the calls. He knew he'd sent emails. He knew he'd worked on campaigns and given presentations. And yet people said they didn't know who he was or said no one showed up on scheduled video calls when he knew he did. Even his browser history could show his logins to the CRM. His use of the video conferencing system, and the VOIP calls were trackable. None of that stuff was manual. It was not fudged. At least not by him. Either he was in the apps, or he wasn't. The digital trail would prove his story to be true.

But Mr. Stuart was well ahead of him. He had already had the IT department pull a browser history for the day. There were no video conferencing logins. The VOIP tool was not started much less utilized to make calls. The only searches that showed up were for social media and local news early in the day. Since then, there was nothing. It was almost like Dave had not even stayed in the office. It looked like he'd done a couple searches and left – or took a nap at his desk. But he wasn't working. Nothing was in the CRM. No digital evidence of his workday existed.

He got fired on the spot. Security confiscated his laptop, company phone, ID, and badge to get into the building. He found himself unemployed. Dave was in shock and confusion as he rode the bus back home. How would he tell Shelley? What would he tell her? *Stupid Mondays.*

He wondered how things always seemed to happen to him. Why did they usually happen without explanation or a cause? Weird things started happening when he began studying physics and mathematics. He figured that he'd skip school tonight. Shelley had a surprise for him; and boy did he have one for her tonight. The only question in his mind was when to tell her. On the bus ride home, he figured she might be mad if he waited to tell her. But he could use the physical and emotional release that he envisioned coming his way. He'd wait until later and tell her before they went to sleep.

When he got home, Shelley wasn't there. He plopped down on the sofa and threw his feet onto the coffee table. He decided to flip through the old picture albums they had. He promised many times to scan them and turn them into a digital album. He envisioned the pictures rotating every few seconds. That way they could enjoy them all without any real effort -- like scrolling through albums. Although the effort of scanning them all impeded him from accomplishing this task. Many of the pictures were only prints with no digital version available. Those older ones would be time consuming to scan and put in some sort of organized digital file. Without a job now, he wondered if he could focus on that and get it off his to-do-list. At least it would help improve her mood after the fact. The initial pain and confusion would lead to outbursts. His hard work on this project would help. Then he could lean into getting a new and better paying job. It would help keep both of them pre-occupied a little bit and off the subject of his firing.

Shelley's expressions that morning had gotten him reminiscing about the past. Now he kind of wanted to see the older pictures rotating and popping up in front of him in a digital frame. This was definitely going to be his plan. He'd start on that the next morning. His first full day of unemployment would be a full day of working on this project alone. He would need to decompress from the job firing. He could wait a few days or even a week to start applying for jobs. Meanwhile, these pictures brought back good memories. The early days of their relationship were there for the viewing. Happier times. Times when 'stud muffin' was a regular utterance.

While he flipped through the albums though, he noticed that there were no pictures of him. Somewhere else, he thought. He finished with the albums in the living room. Then he finished the ones he knew about on the bookshelf in the den. He was in none of them. He was quite upset. This was turning out to be one hell of a day. Even the wedding pictures were solos of Shelley or ones with her maids of honor or her parents. Where were his pictures?

He began to search the house for a possible hiding place. She had to be playing some game on him. She'd put together an album only with photos of him and hid it somewhere. She said she had a surprise. Could that be it? Instead of what he thought and hoped. She'd done something special with the pictures. If he was lucky; it was both. *Why only my pictures? This was perplexing.*

As he progressed in his search for pictures, he noticed none of his stuff was around either. He checked all over the house and couldn't find even a piece of his clothing. None of his books. None of his schoolwork or notebooks. Nothing was visible anywhere.

She's packed me up and is kicking me out. "Could that be her surprise?" He said aloud as he became more desperate and confused. This was not the evening he had been anticipating. It was looking like another nail in the coffin of a terrible day. *Stud muffin indeed,* he thought. *It was all some crazy set up. In bad taste at that. And on the worst possible day for it.* Kenny Rogers lyrics for Lucille started running through his mind.

"Worst Monday ever." He mumbled to himself.

Shelley was across the street at her best friend Marge's house. They noticed a strange man rummaging around her living room. They watched through the front windows. The curtains were left opened to allow in sunlight during the day. So, they could see this strange man walking around. Shelley got agitated. So, Marge called the police and explained the situation.

When the police arrived, Dave was coming downstairs as he continued to search the house. Shelley and Marge were standing on the sidewalk leading up to the front door. They were at least 10 feet behind the police officer. His partner was standing in front of them for protection. They did not know if this was an armed break-in situation. Opening the front door revealed the stairs going up to the top floor.

"That's him!" Shelley yelled as she pointed at Dave. The view from the front sidewalk was straight and sure. None of them could miss the man walking down the stairs.

"You say he broke into your house, and you don't know him?" The officer standing in front of Shelley and Marge asked her. The other officer stepped into the house to block Dave from any possible attempt at leaving.

While they could all see Dave, he had a higher vantage point and could also see them. He noticed the police officer walking into the house with one hand on his holster. He noticed another officer standing outside with his wife and her best friend behind him.

"Shelley? What's going on?" Dave asked as the police officer directed him to put his hands on the wall and did a quick frisk. Before he knew it, he was being handcuffed.

Police escorted him out of the house and put him into a squad car. Dave stared out the window of the cruiser at his wife who had moved to the side of the yard. The other officer remained between them as a barrier of sorts. Shelley and Marge were holding each other. Scared. Relieved. The officer assured them that this burglar could not get out of the back seat of the squad car. They were safe.

After processing at the station, Dave decided to make a few phone calls. There were no injuries. He cooperated. For all they knew, he was a vagrant who saw an opportunity to rob a house that looked empty. With his first call, he tried his brother Barney; but nobody was home. Then he decided to call his mother.

"Mom, I'm in jail."

"Is that you Barney?"

"No mom, it's me Dave. Look, Shelley is playing some sort of trick on me. How about coming down to the precinct and get me out?"

"I'm sorry, I don't have a son named Dave. You must have a wrong number."

Dave sat there stunned after his mother hung up on him. An officer asked him if he had finished his calls. He nodded his head as if he didn't know what else to do or who else to call. The policeman that escorted him to his cell asked him his name again.

"Sir, Dave Raspey is not on file with the DMV. We checked archives and interstate databases as well. We have no record of such a person. Why don't you tell us your real name and make it easier on everybody?"

"But I am Dave Raspey!"

"Have it your way Mr. Raspey. For now, we'll list you as John Doe. We'll find out your real name. In the meantime, you can wait in this cell."

As he sat in his cell, he pondered the events of the day. First Shelley had called him stud muffin and talked about a surprise. He had lost two accounts because people didn't remember him. Other people denied he'd even called. His digital trail at work was gone. Erased. His pictures and personal belongings were gone from his home. His mother didn't know who he was. The official files and records of his life were gone from the DMV and other databases and archives. It was like he didn't exist anymore.

The next morning the police shift changed. The new officer in charge of the headcount noticed one extra person. They made roll call several times. They would count the inmates, compare notes for assignments to each cell. They made additional roll calls and watched and listened for each response. Dave never spoke. None of the staff knew who he was or recognized him. They focused on Dave.

"Who are you and why are you here? How did you get into the cell? And why?"

He repeated his name. He told them about the arrest in his own house the night before.

"Sir we have no record of you. Not even under a 'John Doe' name. We are going to have to release you sir."

"Do you have someone who can pick you up?" A police sergeant asked. He was trying to figure out how to handle the discharge of a person with no paperwork.

"You could try my wife, Shelley." He said as he grabbed a pen and sticky pad and wrote down her number.

The sergeant dialed the number Dave had given him. It was a disconnected number. It made a weird series of beeps and issued a standard message from the telephone company. It was no longer in service.

"Sir, that number is invalid. Do you have another one?"

"No." Dave said realizing he was getting nowhere. His mother had already hung up on him. His brother hadn't answered. But based on everything else that had happened in the last 24 hours, he didn't expect he would answer today. "No. No I don't." He reiterated.

"Well, if there is no one to pick you up, we can drop you off somewhere if you want."

Dave thought about it for a moment. He knew where the emergency house key was hidden outside. He figured he could try to go back home to where this all started. So, he gave the officer an address. The sergeant called dispatch to have a squad car run him over to the address and get rid of him.

When they got to the house, Dave was glad to see it was still there. He thanked the officer who drove him out and walked up to the door. It found it locked. He pulled out his key to open it. The key wouldn't fit. *'She's changed the locks already'* he thought to himself. *It figures. Disconnected phone. Changed locks. Monday rolls into Tuesday as if they were one and the same.*

He started walking around the house looking for a window that might be open. They were all locked. He could see into the house through one of the side windows where the curtain was not closed. It was empty. Nothing was in it. It was absolutely empty.

He stood staring through the window. Incredulity overwhelmed him. As he stood, a neighbor called out to him from over the fence separating the yards.

"They're gone."

Dave turned around to look at a neighbor he didn't know. He didn't get out to the back yard or the sides of the house very often. He had always hired people to maintain the yard. Landscapers came and went. The front yard was pretty much all he knew of this neighborhood and his neighbors. He would nod and wave as people walked by or as he jogged around. But he didn't know anyone and made no attempt to get to know anyone. Work and Shelley were his life. The rest was noise. When he was home, he was home to rest or spend time with Shelley. He was too introverted to care about the neighbors.

"Packed up and moved after old man McDermott died. I guess they couldn't handle living in the same house. Are you related to them?"

McDermott? He remembered that name. He and Shelley had bought the house from the estate of the McDermott's. The old man's kids were at the closing because the wife was already in stages of dementia. The kids had taken control of everything. But that was years ago. He remembered hearing something about the owner's death. But the details at the time didn't matter and he couldn't remember them now.

"Uh, yes."

"I was out of pocket hiking in the mountains and when I got back, I heard that he had died. I came as fast as I could. I didn't know they had already left. I should have called first." Dave continued. He wasn't sure what to say. But identification as a potential burglar again today would not do. That wasn't an experience he wanted to repeat. So, he thought on his feet and pretended to be part of the family.

The neighbor bought it. He nodded. "Sorry about your loss. Old man McDermott was a great guy. That massive heart attack shocked everyone. And with Mrs. McDermott's poor health, I guess the kids whisked her away. I hear the house is going to be put on the market soon. They've hired a realtor even though they haven't put up a sign or started staging yet."

"I guess they need to take care of Mrs. McDermott and get her settled in first. I'll have to make some calls around the family and see what else I can find out." Dave answered as he continued to build upon his own lies.

The neighbor continued talking. But Dave walked away even though the neighbor was trying to get his attention. He started walking across town. When he got to the town square, he sat down on a bench to rest and think. The events had been so random and so backwards. He needed time to process things.

There was a cacophony of white noise. There were children playing. Dogs were barking. Traffic horns piped in from time to time. The clock tower chimed. He tuned it all out while he tried to rewind all the events of the last day and a half in his mind. Everything was backwards. Like he'd entered some sort of mental black hole or was traveling faster than the speed of light. His brain seemed to be traveling that fast. Neurons and synapses were firing as thoughts and images played across his mind at warp speed. *Einstein was right. Time is relative. Time in fact does go on, even if it goes backwards.* As Dave dosed off to sleep in the warm sun on the park bench, he could hear a car going by blaring its music for all to hear. It was playing 'Nowhere Man' by The Beatles.

As he slept, he dreamt and wondered if he'd even wake up at all. Exactly how much more could even disappear? His customers forgot him. His wife forgot him. His mom forgot him. His house was empty. His brother was gone. Years were gone. And he had been looking into a house he hadn't bought yet. He could only ponder the possibilities now. But his marriage had been bland for a while. He hated his job. His mom was old. Perhaps the universe was giving him a chance to start over.

10 THE PENNY FARTHING

After seeing one chained up outside of Jay's Bagels, Tommy remembered his grandfather had kept a Penny Farthing bike in his barn. He hadn't seen it or thought about it in years. No one had touched or moved it since he was a child. With this sighting, he wondered what happened to the bike after his grandfather died and his estate auctioned.

The stories about the haunted bike passed from generation to generation. In the original story, a boy named Bobby had stolen the new fancy big-wheeled Penny Farthing only to disappear without a trace. The bike turned up abandoned on the side of a country road. No signs of Bobby were ever found. His cries were still heard occasionally in conjunction with a cold evening breeze. Legends said that Bobby's ghost haunted the bike and warned people to stay away from it. The legend was so prevalent that everyone referred to that 5 mile stretch of rural route 94 as Bobby's Ghost Road instead of it's official name of Huddle Road.

As a kid, Tommy's grandfather had told the story to him and his friends one summer night around a bonfire. His friends decided to test the bike. They intended to determine if it remained haunted or was only the stuff of tall tales.

With Tommy out of town one weekend, his friends went into action. Brian, Sophie, Jan, and Frank got together on a gloomy summer night and crept quietly into the barn owned by Tommy's grandfather. When they opened the barn doors, they creaked as if the old building was moaning. A cold wind swept through the air. The hairs on the back of their necks tingled in anticipation and dread as an uneasy feeling washed over them. They hesitated and looked at each other. Trying to impress Sophie, Frank walked forward determined to put on a good show of bravery.

As they all moved forward, dust danced in the beams of their flashlights. The effect cast eerie shadows on the walls. The wind still moving through the barn seemed to whisper to them in words they couldn't quite make out. Field mice, startled by the light and unexpected visitors scurried across the ground and out of the barn making Jan scream when she saw them.

Everyone's hearts were beating rapidly with the sudden movement and scream. But Brian's flashlight caught a flicker of a reflection. The bicycle, the ancient Penny Farthing, sat propped against a bale of hay. It cast a sinister-looking silhouette as the dusty air played tricks with their vision.

Sophie stepped forward first. Brian and Frank held the lights steady as Jan stepped backwards scanning the floor for more mice. Sophie reached out for the bike as shivers ran down her spine. This was the moment of truth. She grabbed the big front wheel and started to pull it away from the bale.

The boys encouraged her to get on it and ride it out through the open barn door and into the field and down the dirt road beyond. Positioning herself behind the bike, Sophie straddled the rear wheel while holding on to the handle bars. She put her left foot on the lower step and prepared to mount the bike.

Frank came over to help hold up the bike from the left side as Sophie worked to mount it. She pushed the bike forward like it was a skateboard to get some momentum and brought her right leg up to the higher step. She swung herself up and onto the seat as the bike moved slightly forward.

Frank let go as Sophie grasped the handlebars and moved her feet into the pedals. As soon as her right foot found the pedal and she started to move the bike forward of her own momentum, a shock ran through her body. An icy grip latched on to her hands and feet.

"You belong to me now."

The voice was audible to them all. Frank spun around looking for someone. Brian and Jan immediately ran out of the barn. Sophie was in sheer panic trying to stop the bike and get off of it. But her hands and feet were firmly bound.

A cold ghostly force blew like a gale wind through the barn propelling the bike forward even as Sophie struggled to free herself. Frank got knocked to the ground in the process. The bike rolled out of the barn with Sophie. It caught up with Brian and Jan. The freezing wind pushed them forward so that their running looked more like stumbling and falling at full speed. Then it knocked them to the ground as well.

As fast as the wind came, it subsided. Frank came out of the barn shaken by his experience. Seeing Brian and Jan on the ground, he ran over to them. Everyone was none the worse for wear. But Sophie was gone. She and the Penny Farthing had disappeared down the dirt road.

The abandoned bike turned up by the side of the road a couple miles from the barn. Frank, Jan, and Brian retold the story to the police and friends. No one ever believed them. Sophie was never found. The open cold case helped the legends of the haunted Penny Farthing grow. After its return to the barn, it remained untouched. Tommy hadn't thought of it for years. No one had dared to enter the barn again.

Thinking back, he remembered Frank's parents put him into therapy. Jan and Brian both eventually moved away. Tommy didn't have contact with any of them. Now he stood and looked at this modern version of the Penny Farthing bike as a cold breeze chilled his bones.

ABOUT THE AUTHOR

Brýn Grover writes from the eerie shadows of the Old Dominion where the Bunnyman roams. His short stories blend the weird and the unusual with unsettling horror. As a lifelong fan of B-movies and drive-in nightmares, he channels his passion for the macabre into tales that linger long after the final page.

His collections have included *The Golem and Other Stories, All Things End?,* and *Jamie's Closet.* His writings have also appeared in *Dark Corners of the Old Dominion* and *Devour the Rich.* His award-winning poetry has appeared in multiple places. His latest poetry collection *Catacombs: A Collection of Horror Poetry,* combines his poetic style with his fascination of all things horror.

When not writing, he explores abandoned places, indulges in dark tourism, and pursues his fascination with graveyards and cemeteries as an unapologetic taphophile.

www.ingramcontent.com/pod-product-compliance
Lightning Source LLC
Chambersburg PA
CBHW072045170626
46811CB00008B/3174